This edition published by Parragon Books Ltd in 2014 and distributed by

Parragon Inc.
440 Park Avenue South, 13th Floor
New York, NY 10016
www.parragon.com

Copyright © Parragon Books Ltd 2013–2014

ISBN 978-1-4723-5204-0

Printed in China

The Wizard of Oz

Based on the original story by L. Frank Baum
Retold by Claire Sipi

Illustrated by Holly Clifton-Brown

PaRragon

Bath • New York • Singapore • Hong Kong • Cologne • Delhi
Melbourne • Amsterdam • Johannesburg • Shenzhen

Dorothy was an orphan. She lived in a small, one-room house in the middle of the vast, treeless Kansas prairies, with her Uncle Henry, who was a farmer, and Aunt Em, Henry's wife. There were no other houses for miles in this bleak, gray landscape.

Uncle Henry and Aunt Em had a big bed in one corner and Dorothy a little bed in another corner. There was no proper cellar—just a small, dark hole, dug in the middle of the floor, reached by a trapdoor and ladder. This was the cyclone cellar, where the family could go in case one of those great whirlwinds arose, mighty enough to crush any building in its path.

The only thing that kept Dorothy, a merry little girl, from growing as gray as her surroundings was Toto. He was a little black dog with long, silky hair and twinkly black eyes. Dorothy loved him dearly and played with him all day long.

Today, however, they were not playing. Uncle Henry looked anxiously at the sky, as he listened to the low wail of the winds rippling across the flat prairie from the north and south. Suddenly, he jumped up.

"There's a cyclone coming, Em," he shouted. "Go to the cellar with Dorothy, and I'll go look after the livestock."

One glance at the sky told Aunt Em of the danger close at hand. "Quick, Dorothy!" she cried, as she climbed down the ladder into the small, dark hole.

Dorothy grabbed Toto and started to follow Aunt Em. The house was shaking so hard that she lost her footing and sat down suddenly upon the floor.

A strange thing then happened.

The house whirled around two or three times and rose slowly through the air like a balloon, leaving the prairie and Aunt Em behind. It was caught in the center of the cyclone, where the wind is still. The pressure of the surrounding wind pushed the house higher and higher, until it was sitting at the very top of the cyclone and was carried miles away.

For hours, the house floated on the swirling wind. The swaying motion and darkness were strangely peaceful. Dorothy crawled across the floor with Toto and climbed onto her bed. Soon, with the gentle rocking, she fell fast asleep.

Bang! Dorothy woke with a start. The house was no longer moving, and sunshine flooded into the little room. She sprang from the bed and, with Toto at her heels, ran outside. With a cry of amazement, Dorothy drank in the beautiful sights that met her eyes: green grass, trees bearing fruits, banks of gorgeous flowers, brightly colored birds swooping over a gurgling brook.

Out of the corner of her eye, Dorothy noticed a strangely dressed group of people walking toward her. She could tell they were adults, but none of them were taller than Dorothy herself. There were three old men and one much older, white-haired, wrinkly-faced woman.

"Welcome, most noble Sorceress, to the land of the Munchkins. We are grateful to you for having killed the Wicked Witch of the East and for setting our people free from her evil rule," said the woman.

Dorothy looked confused. "You're very kind, but I haven't killed anyone."

The woman laughed. "Well, your house did! Look!"

Dorothy turned and saw two legs with ruby slippers on the ends of them, sticking out from under a corner of the house.

"Oh, dear!" she cried.

The woman smiled reassuringly. "Don't worry. She was one of the two wicked witches who rule in our Land of Oz. The other lives in the West. I'm the Good Witch of the North, and the other good witch rules in the South. But even more powerful than us witches is the Great Oz, a wizard who lives in the Emerald City."

Dorothy felt overwhelmed by all this talk of witches and wizards, and she began to sob. "I must get home to my uncle and aunt," she said. "Can you help me?"

The Good Witch shook her head. "Only the Great Oz can help you. You must travel to the Emerald City. Oz is a dangerous land, but my kiss will keep you from harm." She kissed Dorothy on the forehead, then handed her the Wicked Witch's ruby slippers. "Wear these. They have special magical powers. And now, just follow the yellow-brick road."

And with that, she disappeared in a puff of smoke.

"Oh!" gasped Dorothy in surprise, and she turned toward the Munchkin men. They bowed low and wished her a pleasant journey before walking away through the trees.

Alone now, Dorothy called to Toto and went into the house to prepare for her journey to the Emerald City. She put on her clean blue-and-white checked dress, took a little basket and filled it with bread, laying a white cloth over the top. Then she looked down at her feet, noticing her old and worn shoes.

"I wonder if these will fit me?" she said, picking up the ruby slippers and remembering the Good Witch's words. The shoes fitted her as if they had been her own.

"Come along, Toto," she said, locking the door of the house. "We'll go to the Emerald City and ask the Great Oz how to get back to Kansas again."

Dorothy began to follow the road paved with yellow bricks. After she had gone several miles, she thought she would stop to rest by a cornfield. Just beyond the fence, she saw a scarecrow, placed high on a pole to keep the birds from the ripe corn.

As Dorothy gazed at the strange, painted face, she was surprised to see one of its eyes slowly wink at her. She climbed over the fence to take a closer look.

"Good day," said the Scarecrow in a rather husky voice.

"Did you speak?" Dorothy asked in wonder.

"Certainly!" said the Scarecrow. "I'm not feeling well. If you would be so kind as to help me off this pole, I would feel much better."

Dorothy reached up and lifted the Scarecrow off the pole. Being stuffed with straw, he was quite light!

"Thank you," sighed the Scarecrow. "I feel like a new man! And may I ask who you are, kind young lady? And where are you going?"

"I'm Dorothy," Dorothy replied, and she started to tell the Scarecrow her strange story.

"Who is the Great Oz?" asked the Scarecrow.

"Don't you know?" Dorothy replied in surprise.

The Scarecrow bowed his head sadly. "No. I don't know anything. You see, I'm stuffed, so I have no brains at all."

"Oh," said Dorothy, "I'm awfully sorry for you."

"Do you think," the Scarecrow began, "if I go to Emerald City with you, that Oz will give me some brains?"

"I don't know," replied Dorothy, "but you can come with me, if you like."

The Scarecrow smiled. "I do not want people to call me a fool because my head is full of straw. I don't mind the rest of me being stuffed with straw because I cannot get hurt, but if I don't have a brain, how will I ever know anything?"

Dorothy felt very sorry for the Scarecrow. "If you come with me, I'll ask Oz to do all he can for you."

They walked back to the yellow-brick road.

"Thank you," said the Scarecrow, gratefully. "Let me carry your basket, for I can't get tired."

Dorothy handed her new friend her basket, and they set off on their journey.

Toward evening, the travelers came to a great forest. It was dark under the trees, and they stumbled along the path.

"Let's stop if we find a house or somewhere to pass the night," whispered Dorothy.

The Scarecrow stopped. "I can see a little cottage to the left," he said.

He led Dorothy through the trees. The cottage was empty, so they went inside. Dorothy lay down on a bed of dried leaves with Toto and soon fell into a sound sleep. The Scarecrow, who was never tired, stood in a corner and waited patiently for morning.

When Dorothy awoke, the sun was already shining through the trees. After a quick breakfast of bread and a drink of water from a nearby stream, Dorothy called to Toto and the Scarecrow.

"Let's get on our way," she said, anxious to get to the Emerald City as quickly as possible to see if Oz could help her get home again.

They had just stepped onto the yellow-brick road, when they heard a deep groan nearby.

"What was that?" Dorothy asked timidly.

"I cannot imagine," replied the Scarecrow. "Shall we go and look?"

They followed the groaning sound back into the forest. Something shiny caught Dorothy's eye, and she stopped with a little cry of surprise.

Standing beside a partly chopped tree, with an uplifted ax in his hands, was a man made entirely of tin. He stood perfectly motionless, as if he could not stir at all.

Dorothy looked at him in amazement. "Did you groan?" she asked.

"Yes," mumbled the Tin Man, through lips that were nearly rusted together. "I did. I've been groaning for more than a year, and no one has heard me before or come to help me."

Dorothy was moved by the sad voice. "What can I do for you?" she asked softly.

"Go to my cottage over there, and get an oil can and oil my joints," he answered. "They are rusted so badly that I cannot move them at all."

Dorothy went into the little cottage. She found the oil can, and returning quickly, she gently oiled all the Tin Man's joints and his mouth.

"Ah, thank you," he sighed, once he could move again. "You've saved my life. How did you happen to be here?"

"We're on our way to see the Great Oz to ask if he can send me back to Kansas and give the Scarecrow a brain."

The Tin Man appeared to think deeply for a moment. Then he said, "Do you suppose Oz could give me a heart?"

"Why, I guess so," Dorothy answered. "It will be a pleasure to have your company on our journey. But surely, you must already have a heart?"

"Well, I did have a heart once ..." replied the Tin Man, and he started to tell his new friends his sad story, as they continued along the path through the forest.

"I was once an ordinary Munchkin boy, and I was in love with a beautiful Munchkin girl. We were going to get married. Unfortunately, the girl lived with an old woman who didn't want her to marry anyone. She was very lazy, and she wanted the girl to remain with her to cook and clean. So the old woman went to the Wicked Witch of the East and got her to cast a spell on me to prevent me marrying the girl."

The Tin Man sighed and then continued. "She enchanted my ax so that it gradually cut off all my limbs and then my head! I went to a tinsmith, and luckily, he was able to make me new legs, arms, and a head out of tin. I could move as long as I kept myself oiled.

"Not satisfied, the Witch made my ax slip and cut my body in two halves. The tinsmith made me a new body, but he couldn't give me a heart. I lost all my love for the Munchkin girl and did not care whether I married her or not.

"One day, I forgot to oil myself. I got caught in a rainstorm and rusted where you found me," finished the Tin Man. "I've had a lot of time to think. While I was in love, I was the happiest man on earth. But no one can love without a heart. If Oz gives me a heart, I will go back to the Munchkin maiden and marry her."

"Let's hope the wizard can help you both," sighed Dorothy, as the Tin Man and Scarecrow chatted about whether it was better to have a heart or a brain.

Dorothy was just wondering when they'd get out of the forest, when a terrible roar made her stop dead in her tracks. A huge lion bounded onto the path.

With one blow of his huge paw, the Lion sent the Scarecrow spinning over to the edge of the path. Then he struck the Tin Man with his sharp claws. The Tin Man toppled over, but much to the Lion's surprise, his claws made no marks on the shiny man's body.

Toto started barking and ran toward the Lion. The great beast opened his mouth to bite the little dog, but before he could snap his jaws, Dorothy, fearing Toto would be killed and heedless of the danger to herself, rushed forward and slapped the Lion on his nose as hard as she could. The Lion whimpered and started shaking as he backed away.

"Don't you dare bite Toto!" Dorothy screamed. "You ought to be ashamed of yourself, a big beast like you, biting a poor little dog! You're nothing but a big coward!"

"I'm sorry!" cried the Lion, hanging his head in shame. "I try to be brave by acting tough. But it's useless. I can't help being afraid."

"What's happened to make you like this?" huffed Dorothy, as she helped the Tin Man to his feet and patted the Scarecrow back into shape again.

"It's a mystery," replied the Lion. "I'm not brave, even though the lion is supposed to be the King of Beasts. I learned early in life that if I roared very loudly, every living thing was frightened and got out of my way."

The Lion wiped a tear from his eye. "If only I could have some courage, my life wouldn't be so unbearable!"

"Perhaps the Great Oz can give you some courage," said the Scarecrow. "Come with us. I'm going to ask him for some brains."

"And I'm going to ask him for a heart," added the Tin Man.

So, once more, the little group set off upon their journey. What adventures the friends had that day while traveling through the forest! They had to flee from many strange creatures and cross huge ditches that blocked their path on the yellow-brick road.

Finally, they came to a broad river at the edge of the forest. Dorothy feasted on nuts and fruit before curling up with Toto. Feeling safe with her new band of friends, she fell fast asleep.

Dorothy and her friends awoke the next morning refreshed and full of hope. The Tin Man made a raft from logs for them to cross the broad river.

They climbed onto the raft, and things were going well until they reached the middle of the river. The swift current swept the raft downstream, farther and farther away from the yellow-brick road on the other side.

"Oh, what a disaster!" cried the Scarecrow. "We must get to the Emerald City." He put his pole into the water to try and stop the raft, but it got stuck. The Scarecrow was left clinging to the pole in the middle of the river, while the raft with the others floated off without him.

"Oh, no, what are we going to do?" cried Dorothy.

"Hold onto my tail," cried the Lion, as he jumped into the river, "and I'll swim to shore with the raft."

After a hard struggle, the Lion reached the shore.

"We must get back to the yellow-brick road and save the Scarecrow," said Dorothy.

Suddenly, they saw the Scarecrow. A kind stork had lifted him from his pole in the river and was dropping him on the bank by a field of poppies.

The friends were delighted and set off through the poppy field.

"I feel so sleepy," yawned the Lion.

"Me too!" said Dorothy. "The smell of these flowers is too much ...."

She swayed and then suddenly dropped to the ground. Within seconds, the Lion and Toto fell next to Dorothy. They were soon all fast asleep. Only the Tin Man and the Scarecrow were left standing.

"It must be these flowers," cried the Tin Man. "Quick, help me carry them away from here." The two friends realized that the flowers were poisonous to humans and animals.

As they were trying to figure out how they could carry the heavy Lion, a large wildcat raced past them, chasing a field mouse. Without thinking, the Tin Man struck out with his ax, killing the wildcat immediately.

"Thank you so much!" squeaked the mouse. "You saved my life. I'm the Queen of the Field Mice. Is there anything I can do for you?"

"We need to get our friend the Lion out of this field," said the Tin Man. "Can you help us?"

The Queen summoned all her mice, and they helped the travelers pull the sleeping Lion out of the field.

"Thank you for helping us," cried the Tin Man.

"You saved my life," replied the Queen. "If you ever need us again, just call out, and we will come to your assistance. Goodbye!"

As soon as Dorothy, Toto, and the Lion woke up, the travelers continued on their journey.

When they finally reached the Emerald City, they saw a huge wall surrounding the city. Amidst its dazzling emeralds, they found a big gate. Dorothy rang the bell next to it. The gate swung open, and they all passed through.

A little man stood before them, dressed in green.

"What do you wish in the Emerald City?" he asked.

"We came here to see the Great Oz," replied Dorothy.

The man stared at Dorothy. "I am the Guardian of the Gates. If you wish to see the Great Oz, I must take you to his Palace."

Dorothy and her friends were shown to rooms in the palace and were told they would be collected, one by one, to see Oz.

Dorothy was the first to be taken to the wizard's Throne Room. Above a chair in the middle of the room floated a giant head. Dorothy gazed upon it in wonder and fear.

"I am Oz, the Great and Terrible. Who are you, and why do you seek me?" said the floating head.

Nervously, Dorothy replied, "I am Dorothy, the Small and Meek. I have come to you for help." And she told Oz her story.

The floating head nodded. "Before I can help you, you must kill the Wicked Witch of the West. Now go, and do not ask to see me again until you have done your task."

With a heavy heart, Dorothy went back to her friends and told them what had happened. One by one, the Tin Man, Scarecrow, and Lion were all told the same thing by the great wizard.

"What shall we do now?" wept Dorothy.

"There is only one thing we can do," replied the Lion. "We must find the Wicked Witch and destroy her!"

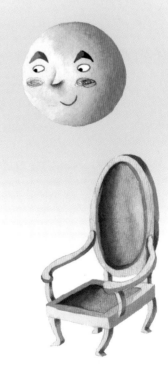

The next day, Dorothy and her friends left the dazzling Emerald City, following the advice of the gatekeeper: "Keep to the West, where the sun sets, and you cannot fail to find the Wicked Witch."

The Wicked Witch of the West had eyes as powerful as a telescope, and she could see everywhere in the land. She spied the little group of friends and was angry to find them in her country.

"I will destroy them," she cackled, and with a blast upon a silver whistle, she summoned a pack of fierce wolves.

The wolves attacked the travelers, but the brave Tin Man, wielding his ax, killed them all, saving his friends.

The Witch was furious. With another blast of her whistle she sent a flock of vicious crows to attack the little group. This time, the courageous Scarecrow fought and killed all the crows. She stamped her feet in anger.

"I will summon the Winged Monkeys with the power of the Golden Cap," she screeched. "This time they will not escape!"

The Golden Cap was charmed, and whoever owned it could call three times upon the Winged Monkeys to help them.

The Winged Monkeys were too powerful for the little band of travelers, and the friends were captured and taken to the Witch's castle.

When the Witch saw the Good Witch of the North's kiss of protection on Dorothy's forehead, even she was afraid to touch the girl. Instead, she forced Dorothy to work in the kitchen of her castle, cooking and cleaning, and plotted how to get the magic ruby slippers that Dorothy still wore on her feet.

Several weeks went past. Then one day, the Witch tripped Dorothy as she was cleaning the kitchen floor, and Dorothy lost one of her shoes. The Witch grabbed it. "Soon the other one will be mine!" she cackled gleefully.

Dorothy was furious. "You are a wicked creature!" she screamed at the Witch. "You have no right to take my shoe from me."

The Witch just laughed, which made Dorothy even angrier. Dorothy picked up the bucket of water next to her and threw it over the Witch.

"No! See what you have done!" screamed the Witch. "In a minute, I shall melt away!"

Dorothy watched in horror as the Witch disappeared into a puddle of water. With a trembling hand, Dorothy grabbed the ruby slipper from the puddle, which was all that remained of the Witch, and put it on. Then she raced out of the kitchen to find her friends.

With much joy in their hearts, Dorothy and her friends set free everyone the Witch had enslaved over the years.

Before they left the castle, Dorothy went to the Witch's cupboard to fill her basket with food for the journey back to Oz. Lying on one of the shelves was the Golden Cap. Dorothy picked it up.

"This is pretty," she said, putting the Cap on. It fitted her perfectly, so she decided to keep it— after all, the Witch wouldn't need it now! Dorothy, however, didn't know it had magical powers.

With her basket full, Dorothy and her friends began their return journey to the Emerald City.

"I shall get my brains!" cried the Scarecrow.

"I shall get my heart!" laughed the Tin Man.

"I shall get my courage!" roared the Lion.

"And I shall get back to Kansas!" sighed Dorothy, clapping her hands.

Days went by, and the travelers began to wonder if they would ever get back to the Emerald City. They couldn't see the yellow-brick road any more, just field after field disappearing into the distance.

"We have surely lost our way," grumbled the Scarecrow. "I shall never get my brains now."

Dorothy sighed. "We could call the field mice." She turned to the field, shouting at the top of her voice, "Dear mice, please help us!"

Within a few minutes, an army of small mice appeared. "We've lost our way," Dorothy explained.

The Queen mouse looked at Dorothy. "The City is a great way off. Why don't you use the charm of the Cap and call the Winged Monkeys? They will carry you there in less than an hour."

"What charm?" queried Dorothy.

The Queen explained, and soon Dorothy and her friends were being carried back to the Emerald City by the Winged Monkeys.

After the friends had been back in the Emerald City for over a week, the wizard still refused to see them.

"I'm going to find out what is going on," said Dorothy, and she ran past the guard into the wizard's palace. Sitting in the vast throne room was a small old man. Dorothy was crushed. There was no Great Oz. He was just an ordinary man.

"I'll never get home now," sobbed Dorothy. "You broke all your promises!"

"I'm truly sorry," sighed the little old man. He gestured to Dorothy's friends to join him, and he told them his story. He used to work in a circus in the city of Omaha. One day, the hot-air balloon he was in accidentally floated away. When it eventually landed in Oz, the people thought he was a great wizard, and he was too scared to tell them otherwise.

"Can't you give me brains?" asked the Scarecrow.

"You don't need them. You are learning something every day," said Oz. "Look at yourselves, all of you, you have already got what you are seeking— brains, heart, and courage. You've stuck by each other and helped each other and given each other the love of friendship."

The Tin Man, Scarecrow, and Lion looked at each other and smiled.

"But how will I get home?" whispered Dorothy.

"You must go to see Glinda the Good Witch of the South," Oz replied.

"Dorothy, you have helped us get what we wanted and made us so happy," said the Tin Man. "We will help you find Glinda."

So, once again, the group of friends set out on another long and difficult journey. But with their newfound courage, love, and knowledge, they finally arrived at Glinda's palace.

Dorothy told the Good Witch her story.

Glinda leaned forward and kissed the little girl before her. "All you have to do is click the heels of your ruby slippers together three times and command them to carry you wherever you wish to go," she said.

Dorothy hugged her friends tightly.

"Thank you," she whispered. "I'll never forget you." And with tears in her eyes, she clicked her heels three times.

"Take me home to Aunt Em!"